Jack and the Beanstalk

WRITTEN BY ROSEMARY WELLS
ILLUSTRATED BY NORMAN MESSENGER

DORLING KINDERSLEY
London • New York • Moscow • Stuttgart

LONG AGO AND
FAR AWAY
there lived a
little boy named Jack.
One day a giant reached
right down out of the clouds and
plucked up Jack's father, leaving
only Jack and his mother,
hungry and alone
in the world.

A DORLING KINDERSLEY BOOK

To Jack - NM

First published in Great Britain in 1997 by Dorling Kindersley Limited,
9 Henrietta Street, London WC2E 8PS

4 6 8 10 9 7 5 3

Visit us on the World Wide Web at
http://www.dk.com

Text copyright © 1997 Rosemary Wells
Illustrations copyright © 1997 Norman Messenger

A CIP catalogue record for this book is available from the British Library.

ISBN 0-7513-7038-X

Colour reproduction by Dot Gradations
Printed and bound by Tien Wah Press, Singapore

After a year his mother told young Jack, "We have not a penny left. Take our cow, Bessie, to market. Sell her for as much money as you can get."

On the road to market an old man stopped and admired Bessie.

"I'll give you a bag of beautiful beans for that cow," he said.

Because he loved the
colours of the beans,
Jack agreed.

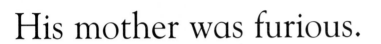

His mother was furious.
"That cow was the last thing of worth
to our names and you've sold her for
five coloured beans! You are as
thick as a brick, Jack!"

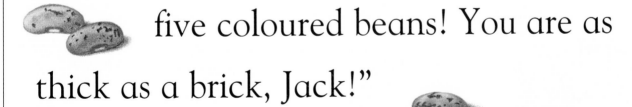

Jack's mother threw the beans out of the window in disgust. Jack went to bed in tears of shame.

But when the sun rose Jack spied a huge green stem right outside his window.

One of the
beans had
sprouted and
its stalk reached
into the clouds.

Up climbed Jack
until he stepped out
from a bean leaf
onto a cloud.

Rising from the cloud was a castle, and
that's where Jack went.

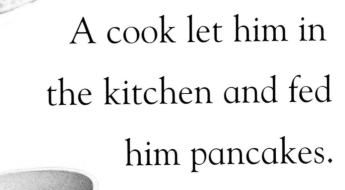

A cook let him in
the kitchen and fed
him pancakes.

"Better hide," she whispered suddenly.
"The giant is just coming for
his breakfast."

The giant ate
three hundred
pancakes.

All the while from some distant part of
the castle came sad singing and the
sound of a harp. Jack hummed to the
song of love and loneliness. He had
heard it somewhere before.

After breakfast the giant clucked and cackled and a hen jumped onto the table. She immediately laid a golden egg in the giant's lap.

The giant played with the egg until he fell asleep. Out sneaked Jack with the hen stuffed under his arm.

Lurching through the pillowy clouds, Jack ran for the beanstalk. He skivvied down it fast as greased lightning.

"My wonderful boy!" said Jack's mother. "One of these golden eggs will buy us all we need for life."

During supper Jack told his mother about the giant's castle and the pancakes. He told her about the harp playing from some distant room.

"Sing the song the harpist sang!" said Jack's mother. And so Jack sang the song.

"Oh," said his mother. "That is a song your father used to sing while he played his harp with the angel's face. A hundred golden eggs could not make me as happy as one bit of melody from the strings of that harp."

Jack could not bear the sadness in his mother's voice and so at first light he climbed the beanstalk once again.

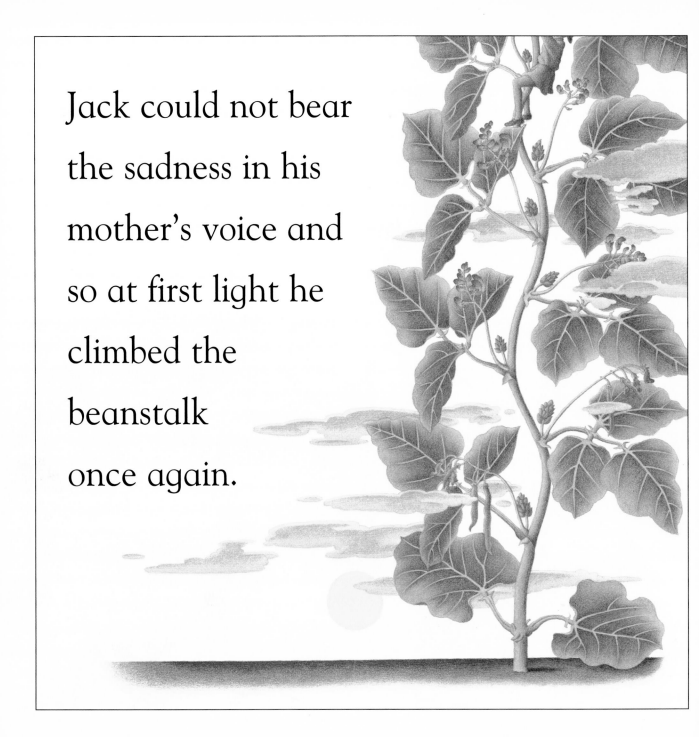

Once again Jack hid while the giant was eating breakfast. When he heard the faraway singing, he crept through a hole beneath the stove and shot into a tunnel under the castle walls.

In darkness Jack crawled, circling ever closer to the mysterious music. At last he reached up and ran his fingers across the strings of his father's harp.

"My brave boy!" whispered his father. "You have come to bring me home."

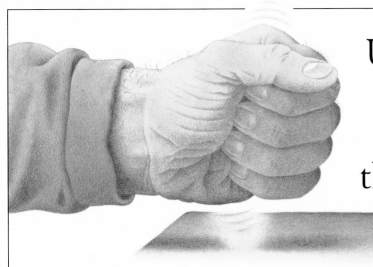

Upstairs the giant banged on the table.

Then he tramped across the floor. Suddenly the cellar was flooded with light.

"I will roast you both on a pig spit and eat you for tea!" roared the giant, catching Jack and his father and the harp in one huge paw of a hand.

Fee fie foe fum...

Then the most curious
thing happened. The
angel on the harp
frowned, and her harp
strings shrilled and
twanged worse than ghosts
of the underworld until
the giant dropped
all of them like
hot potatoes.

Quick as monkeys, Jack and his father scooted between the giant's slow-moving legs. Over the billowing clouds they leapt with the giant a step behind.

Down the beanstalk they twirled until their feet were on mother earth, and then Jack took his hatchet and chopped the beanstalk down.

The giant toppled into the hills and was never heard from again.

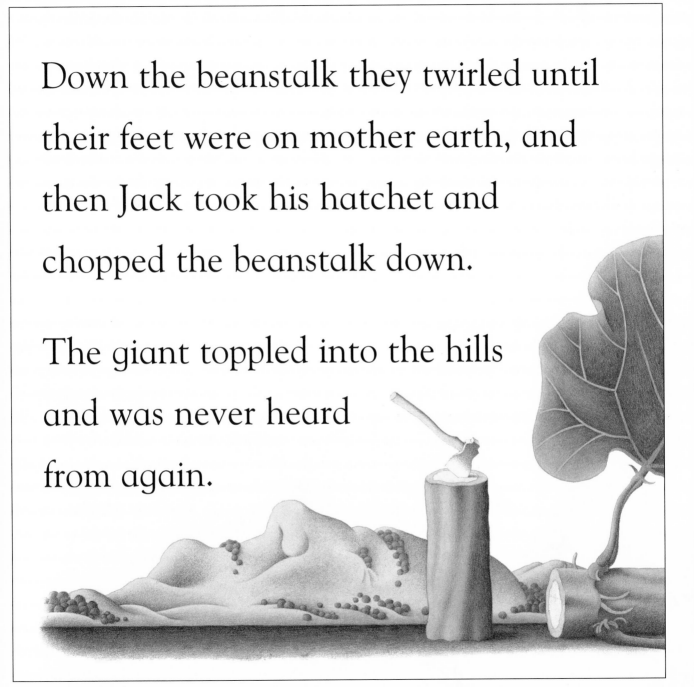

Ever after, Jack's family lived happily. His mother fed marigold seeds and rose petals to the magic hen, and his father taught Jack how to play songs of love and loneliness on the wonderful harp.